GHOSTS GO HAUNTING

HELEN KETTEMAN

ALBERT WHITMAN & COMPANY
CHICAGO, ILLINOIS

PICTURES BY
ADAM RECORD

Library of Congress Cataloging-in-Publication Data

Ketteman, Helen.
The ghosts go haunting / by Helen Ketteman ; illustrations by Adam Record.
pages cm
Summary: "Verses written to the tune of The Ants Go Marching describe
an ever-increasing parade of ghosts, witches, and other spooky creatures
as they haunt a school on Halloween"—Provided by publisher.
1. Children's songs, English—United States—Texts.
[1. Halloween—Songs and music. 2. Songs.] I. Record, Adam, illustrator. II. Title.
PZ8.3.K46Gh 2014
782.42—dc23
[E]
2014000631

Text copyright © 2014 by Helen Ketteman
Illustrations copyright © 2014 by Albert Whitman & Company
Published in 2014 by Albert Whitman & Company
ISBN 978-0-8075-2852-5 (hardcover)
Printed in China.
10 9 8 7 6 5 4 3 2 1 NP 18 17 16 15 14

The design is by Nick Tiemersma.

For more information about Albert Whitman & Company,
visit our web site at www.albertwhitman.com.

M.T. TOMBS
ELEMENTARY

For Chrissy with love–HK

For my two (and one on the way)
adorable kids–AR

SCHOOL

The ghosts go haunting one by one.

Boo! Boo!

The ghosts go haunting one by one.

Boo! Boo!

M.T. TOMBS
ELEMENTARY

The ghosts go haunting one by one.
The principal leaps from his chair and runs,
and they all go screeching
all over thc school
for some Hal-lo-ween fun.

Boo!
Boo!
Boo!
Boo!
Boo!
Boo! Boo! Boo! Boo!

The witches go flying two by two.

Zoom! Zoom!

The witches go flying two by two.

Zoom! Zoom!

The witches go flying two by two.

They ZAP! their milk into witches' brew,

and they all go flying

all over the school

for some Hal-lo-ween fun.

The goblins go groaning three by three.

WOE! WOE!

The goblins go groaning three by three.

WOE! WOE!

The goblins go groaning three by three.
They chase the librarian up a tree,
and they all go groaning
all over the school
for some Hal-lo-ween fun.

WOE! WOE! WOE! WOE!

WOE! WOE!

WOE!

WOE!

The bats go diving four by four.
Flap! Flap!

The bats go diving four by four.
Flap! Flap!

The bats go diving four by four.
They chase the teachers out the front door,
and they all go diving
all over the school
for some Hal-lo-ween fun.

Flap! Flap!
Flap! Flap!
Flap! Flap!
Flap! Flap!

The monsters go stomping five by five.

CLOMP! CLOMP!

The monsters go stomping five by five.

CLOMP! CLOMP!

The monsters go stomping five by five.
They catch the computer repairman alive,
and they take him stomping
all over the school
for some Hal-lo-ween fun.

CLOMP!
CLOMP!
CLOMP!
CLOMP!

Black cats go hissing six by six.

Hiss! Hiss!

Black cats go hissing six by six.

Hiss! Hiss!

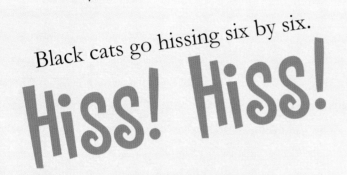

Black cats go hissing six by six.
The school nurse faints like a ton of bricks,
and they all go hissing
all over the school
for some Hal-lo-ween fun.

Hiss!

Hiss!

Hiss!

Hiss!

Hiss!

The spiders go creeping seven by seven.

Creep! Creep!

The spiders go creeping seven by seven.

Creep! Creep!

The spiders go creeping seven by seven.
The lunch ladies run and shout "Good heavens!"
and they all go creeping
all over the school
for some Hal-lo-ween fun.

Creep! Creep!
Creep!
Creep!
Creep! Creep!
Creep! Creep!

The mummies go fright'ning eight by eight.

MOAN! MOAN!

The mummies go fright'ning eight by eight.

MOAN! MOAN!

The mummies go fright'ning eight by eight.
They scare the janitor stiff and straight,
and they all go fright'ning
all over the school
for some Hal-lo-ween fun.

MOAN! MOAN!
MOAN! MOAN!

MOAN! MOAN!
MOAN! MOAN!

The skeletons go rattling nine by nine. Clank! clank!

The skeletons go rattling nine by nine. Clank! Clank!

The skeletons go rattling nine by nine.
The bus driver jumps off the bus to hide,
and they all go rattling
right past the bus
for some Hal-lo-ween fun.

Clank!
Clank!
Clank!
Clank!

The zombies go stumbling ten by ten.
Brains! Brains!

The zombies go stumbling ten by ten.
Brains! Brains!

The zombies go stumbling
ten by ten.
The coach begs for mercy
and then...
and then…

The whole school parties
the rest of the day
for some Hal-lo-ween fun!

HAPPY HALLO

Yay! Yay! Yay! Yay! Yay! Yay! Yay! Yay!

The creatures go marching...

1 X 1

2 X 2

3 X 3

4 X 4

5 X 5

6 X 6

7 X 7

8 X 8

9 X 9

10 X 10